First published in the UK by HarperCollins Children's Books in 2008
1 3 5 7 9 10 8 6 4 2
ISBN 10: 0-00-726157-8
ISBN 13: 978-0-00-726157-4
A CIP catalogue record for this title is available from the British Library.

Printed and bound in Hong Kong

NODDY

Well Done, Noddy!

by Enid Blyton

Contents

THE BICYCLE GREW UNDER THEIR VERY EYES!

POOR BIG-EARS!

ONE fine morning little Noddy was cleaning his car. He had the hose and he was splashing the water all over the bonnet. He sang as he worked.

> *"Dear little car,*
> *You're having a wash,*
> *Out comes the water,*
> *Splishity-splosh.*
> *Soon you'll be clean*
> *And shine like the sun,*
> *And off we will go*
> *For a nice little run!"*

"You sound very merry and bright, Noddy," said the milkman, coming in at the little gate.

Noddy was just going to nod his springy little head when the milkman nodded it for him. He gave it a little tap on top and set Noddy's head nodding madly.

"Yes," said Noddy, nid-nid-nodding as if he would never stop. "Come and look at my new lamps, milkman. I saved up for a long time, and bought them yesterday."

"Wonderful!" said the milkman. "You'll shine as bright as the moon when you go out at night. You're a lucky fellow, Noddy – you've got a dear little house and a garage and a fine car – and a very good friend, too."

"You mean Big-Ears?" said Noddy. "Yes, he's my very best friend and I'd do anything in the world for him. He's always helping me. Perhaps some day I shall be able to help *him*."

"That's the right way to talk," said the milkman. "Just let me give your head one more nod and I must go!"

He set Noddy's head nodding again and then off he went, whistling. Noddy began to dry his car, polishing it as well. He felt very happy.

"Big-Ears is coming to dinner," he thought. "I must go out and get him something nice to eat."

So off he went in his little car, and soon came back with a very large lettuce, six big radishes, two eggs and four jam tarts.

But before he had got the dinner ready somebody came knock-knock-knocking at his little front door.

"Noddy! Noddy! Quick, open the door!"

Noddy opened the door. Mrs Tubby Bear, his next-door neighbour, stood outside, looking most alarmed.

"Oh, Noddy!" she said. "Have you heard the news? Poor Big-Ears was on his bicycle, coming to see you, and round the corner he ran into Jumbo the toy elephant."

"Oh dear! What happened?" cried Noddy. "Tell me quickly."

"Well, Big-Ears fell off and hurt his head. And, oh dear, Jumbo sat down on the bicycle," said Mrs Tubby, two big tears running down her furry nose. "And the bicycle is smashed to bits!"

"What bad news!" said little Noddy, most upset. "Where's Big-Ears? Can I help him? Quick, tell me where he is. I'm his friend, you know. He'll want me."

"Yes, I know," said Mrs Tubby. "You go and get him in your little car, Noddy. Then you can bring him back to your house and look after him until he's better. He's still sitting by the road-side."

Well, it didn't take Noddy long to jump into his little car and go racing off to get Big-Ears.

"Dear, dear Big-Ears!" he thought. "I can't bear him to be hurt. I'm coming, Big-Ears, I'm coming!"

He soon came to the lane where the accident had happened. There was Big-Ears, sitting on a bench, with a big bandage around his head. Sally Skittle had tied it for him. Miss Fluffy Cat was giving him some water to drink.

Jumbo was standing up, trying to pick bits of bicycle off himself. He was grumbling bitterly.

"Coming along at sixty miles an hour like that, never ringing his bell, and me with my shopping basket full of eggs! What next, I'd like to know! I'll NEVER be able to pick all these bits of bicycle off."

But Noddy couldn't bother with Jumbo. He jumped out of his car and ran to Big-Ears.

"Big-Ears! Are you all right? Oh, Big-Ears, what a fright you gave me!"

"I feel a bit funny," said Big-Ears. "And oh, my poor little bicycle! It's smashed to bits! Take me home with you, please, Noddy. Oh, I *am* glad to see you!"

THERE WAS BIG-EARS, SITTING ON A BENCH, WITH A
BIG BANDAGE ROUND HIS HEAD

So Noddy and Miss Fluffy Cat helped poor Big-Ears into the car. Sally Skittle stayed behind to help Jumbo.

"I keep *ringing* somewhere whenever I move," complained Jumbo. "Why do I?"

Sally Skittle gave a squeal of laughter. "Well, you've got the bicycle bell on your tail!" she said. "Each time your tail moves, the bell rings. I'll take it off!"

Jumbo went off, grumbling. Sally Skittle looked at all the bits and pieces of the bicycle. "Oh, what a pity!" she said. "Whatever will Big-Ears do now? What a good thing he has got Noddy for a friend!"

─◦ 2 ◦─

BIG-EARS HAS SOME WORRIES

NODDY drove very carefully so that Big-Ears wouldn't be jolted about. At last they got home, and Noddy helped his friend out of the car.

"Now, you shall stay with me until you're better," he said. "You've so often helped *me*, Big-Ears. It's my turn to help you."

Well, Big-Ears was soon in Noddy's bed. He had on a pair of Noddy's pyjamas, but he couldn't do the buttons up, because he was fatter than Noddy.

"You look strange with your bandage on, and no hat," said Noddy. "Do you mind if I put your

hat on top of the bandage, Big-Ears? You'll look more yourself then."

The doctor soon came. He was a tall teddy bear, with glasses on. He wore a top hat, which made him seem very grand. Noddy was rather scared of him.

"Keep your friend in bed," said Mr Doctor Bear. "Don't let him worry. That's very important. HE MUST NOT WORRY. Good day, little Noddy."

Well, it was all very well to say that Noddy mustn't let Big-Ears worry. How could he stop him?

Big-Ears worried about his little toadstool house.

THE DOCTOR WAS A TALL TEDDY BEAR, WITH GLASSES ON

"Someone may get in and steal my things," he said. "It worries me to think about it. It's all alone and empty."

"I'll see if somebody will go and look after it for you," said Noddy. So he asked Mrs Tubby for her advice.

"I believe Sally Skittle would stay in it until Big-Ears is better," said Mr Tubby. "I know she is having her house painted, and she doesn't like the smell of the paint. You go and ask her."

Well, Sally Skittle was very pleased, especially as Noddy said she could have her three tiny skittle children there as well. They packed up their bags and set off at once.

They soon settled in, and Sally Skittle set her children to work weeding the garden, cleaning the windows and beating the mats.

So that was one worry gone. Then Big-Ears began to worry about the cat.

"Sally Skittle's children might tease her," he said. "I do wish I had old Whiskers here. She'll be so lonely without me. It worries me."

"Oh, Big-Ears! The doctor said you weren't to worry," said Noddy, his head nodding fast. "I'll go and fetch Whiskers. We'll have her here. She's nice. I like her."

So he fetched Whiskers in his car, and Whiskers sat beside Big-Ears all day, and purred so loudly that it sounded like a song.

"I know what she's singing when she purrs,"
said Noddy, and he sang Whiskers' song.

"Stroke me, please,
Because I'm furry,
Pet me, please,
Because I'm purry.
You won't hear
A single mew,
But all day long
I'll purr for you!
Purrr-urrr-urr,
Purrr-RRRRR!"

Big-Ears laughed when Noddy sang all that in a purring voice. But then his whiskered face grew sad again, and Noddy looked at him in alarm.

"Big-Ears! You've thought of another worry! I know you have. Whatever is it this time?"

"No, I shan't tell you," said Big-Ears, and he turned his head away. "It's too big a worry – and I'm afraid that even you can't do anything about it, Noddy."

"I shan't be happy until you tell me," said Noddy. So Big-Ears told him. And it certainly was a VERY BIG WORRY.

3

NODDY GETS AN IDEA

"IT'S about my bicycle," said Big-Ears. "It's all smashed to bits, and I'm sure it can't be mended, can it?"

Noddy shook his head sadly. "No, it can't, Big-Ears. Mr Tubby collected all the bits he could find, but you see, Jumbo is so heavy that he just flattened everything out when he sat on the bicycle."

"Well, that's my Very Big Worry," said Big-Ears. "You see, I've no money saved up, Noddy, so I can't buy a new one. And I live so far away in the wood that I really MUST have a bicycle to ride on to do my shopping."

"Yes, you must," said Noddy, looking very gloomy indeed. "And oh, Big-Ears – I've no money either. I did have some saved up but I used it all to buy new lamps. I think I've got a ha'penny in my money box, but that's all."

He got his money box, and out came the ha'penny. That was all there was. "But don't you worry, now," said Noddy. "I'll think of all sorts of good ideas to get some money to buy you a new bicycle, Big-Ears. I really will."

But it wasn't easy to think of good ideas. Noddy sat on his chair and thought and thought until he fell asleep and fell off his chair too. Oh dear – how did people think of good ideas?

Well, the next day Noddy did have a good idea. He passed by Mr Wobbly Man's garden, and saw the Wobbly Man hard at work there.

"What are you doing?" called Noddy, leaning over the fence.

"I'm planting beans," said Mr Wobbly. "It's a bit difficult because I can't bend over properly

– but I do an extra-big wobble, and plant a bean at each wobble."

"Do the beans grow into bean-plants?" asked Noddy, who really didn't know very much yet.

"Oh yes! And they will grow beans in pods and I shall sell them," said Mr Wobbly. "I sell my plums, too. I planted a plum stone once, and look what a fine plum tree it grew into!" Noddy looked at the plum tree, which was full of blossom. What a wonderful thing! You just planted a bean or a stone and it grew into something that gave you thousands of things like itself!

Noddy went off, thinking hard. Why couldn't *he* grow something like that? He came to the

sweet shop and looked in at the window. He always liked looking into the sweet shop window. It was full of such exciting things.

"Peppermint drops. Oooh!" said Noddy. "Big bull's eyes. Oooh!" And toffees. I wish I had some money. I would take some home to Big-Ears. It might make him forget his worry."

NODDY SAW THE WOBBLY MAN HARD AT WORK

And then a marvellous idea came into Noddy's head, and he nodded so hard that the bell on the end of his hat rang a loud, jingly tune.

"I will buy a peppermint drop, and a bull's eye, and a toffee," he said to himself. "And I will plant them and grow a peppermint drop bush, and a bull's eye tree, and a toffee tree, too. And I can sell them when they are sweet and ripe, and buy a new bicycle for Big-Ears!"

Well, what a wonderful idea! Noddy went home and got the ha'penny out of his money box. The sweet shop woman, who was a very nice little doll, let him have one peppermint drop, one bull's eye and one toffee for the ha'penny.

Noddy planted them all in his garden, and put a label by each one. Aha! This was a fine way to make some money for Big-Ears!

4

NODDY IS CLEVER

THE queer seeds didn't come up the next
day or the next. Noddy kept looking to see.
He asked Big-Ears how long seeds took to grow.

"Oh, a few weeks," said Big-Ears, and Noddy
looked sad. He didn't want Big-Ears to have his
Great Big Worry all that time. He must think of
another Good Idea as quickly as possible.

"Perhaps I could make up a song and sell it,"
he thought. "Big-Ears says I'm good at songs. I'll
go round asking people if they would like me
to make up a nice song about them."

Well, Mr Tubby Bear said he would like a song, so long as Noddy didn't say anything in it about how fat he was. Noddy sat down, his bell jingling, and thought about a Tubby song.

At last he thought of one. Here it is:

> *"Mr Tubby Bear*
> *Has got a lovely grunt.*
> *He keeps it in his middle,*
> *(You press him at the front).*
> *I couldn't call him thin,*
> *But I mustn't call him fat,*
> *And I like him best of all*
> *When he wears his Sunday hat."*

Noddy took it round to Mr Tubby Bear. "Is it worth sixpence?" he asked. "I did my very best."

Mr and Mrs Tubby read it together. "It does rather sound as if I *am* fat," said Mr Tubby, doubtfully. "I like the bit about my lovely grunt, though."

He pressed himself in his middle, and a deep grunt came at once. "That was clever of you to put my grunt into a song, Noddy.

But what do you mean about my Sunday hat? I haven't got one."

"I know," said Noddy. "It just came into the song by itself. But you *would* look nice in a fine Sunday hat, Mr Tubby, and I *would* like you very much in one, I know I would."

"Well, I might buy one then," said Mr Tubby. "I think the song is worth sixpence, so I'll pay you for it. Sing it to me first, though, so that I shall know the tune."

So Noddy sang it in a little high voice, his head nodding in time to the tune. "I shall certainly tell everyone you are a good song-maker," said Mrs Tubby. "Then perhaps you will get some more money."

So she told Miss Toy Bunny, and the next day Miss Bunny came to see Noddy.

"I'd like a song, too," she said, her little nose waffling up and down. "But only a VERY short one because my memory is short and I couldn't learn a *long* one."

"It will be sixpence," said Noddy, and Miss Bunny paid him even before he had thought of her song. He sang her the song the next minute though, so she didn't have to wait long. This is what he sang:

"Waffly nose
And hoppitty feet,
Little Miss Bunny
Is perfectly sweet."

MR AND MRS TUBBY READ THE SONG TOGETHER

Miss Bunny was simply delighted. She went off singing it, and it wasn't long before Noddy became quite famous for his songs. Soon he had written one for Mr Wobbly Man, one for Miss Fluffy Cat, one for Sally Skittle and even one for Jumbo. That took him a long time, though, because Jumbo said he ought to have a big song, because he was so enormous.

Noddy's money box began to fill up! If only his peppermint seeds would grow, and his bull's eyes and toffees, too, what a lot of money he would have! Noddy felt very pleased.

"I'll soon buy a bicycle for Big-Ears!" he thought. "Very, very soon!"

5

A MESSAGE FOR NODDY

BIG-EARS was much better. He was up now, and sitting in a rocking chair that Mrs Tubby Bear had lent him. He still wore a bandage around his head, but it was a much smaller one.

"What I should *really* like would be a ride on my dear old bicycle," he kept saying. "But it's all gone, isn't it, Noddy?"

"Yes, I'm afraid so," said Noddy. "All except the bell, Big-Ears. Sally Skittle brought it back, and I've put it away in a cupboard because I thought it might make you sad to see it."

"Bring it out," said Big-Ears. "I don't like it hidden away. Put it near me and I'll ring it sometimes. It will remind me of my dear old bicycle."

So Noddy got out the bell and put it beside Big-Ears. It still rang beautifully, and whenever Big-Ears wanted little Noddy for anything, he rang his old bicycle bell – r-r-r-r-r-r-r-ring!

Noddy often took passengers in his little car, but he couldn't save much money from the sixpences they gave him because it cost rather a lot to keep Big-Ears as well as himself.

"And I keep buying Big-Ears all sorts of little treats to keep him happy," thought Noddy. "Ice-creams and rosy apples, and a nice book.

I should really be saving the money up for his new bicycle. Oh dear, oh dear, shall I EVER get enough to take him shopping and buy a bicycle just like his old one?"

One day Noddy got a message that was rather exciting. Mrs Tubby brought it.

"Somebody met me when I was out, little Noddy," she said. "It was a messenger from Mr Sailor Doll. He says he's going to sea tomorrow, so will you please drive to his house called Ahoy

Cottage, go round to the back where there is a shed, and collect all the sacks there. Put them in your car, and take them to Red Goblin Corner."

"Very well," said Noddy. "What do I do with them there?"

"Oh, you just leave them for his uncle to collect some time," said Mrs Tubby. "Put them under a bush. You will be paid seven sixpences for doing all that."

"Good gracious me!" said Noddy, pleased. "I shall be very, very rich! I shall put them all in my money box!"

Noddy set off in his little car. He drove to Ahoy Cottage. It was really rather like a steamer, and it had funnels for chimneys, but as

roses grew all around the funnels they looked a bit peculiar.

Noddy went straight round to the back of the cottage. He found the shed. He went in and saw six sacks piled up together, waiting for him.

He dragged them one by one to the little car. At last he had got them all in. Nobody came out to pay him so he thought perhaps Mr Sailor Doll had already left to go to sea. Somebody was

hanging out clothes in the next garden. It was Mrs Minnie Monkey. Noddy didn't know her so he didn't say a word to her. He just got into his car and drove off to Red Goblin Corner.

Nobody was there, so Noddy dragged the sacks out of his car and put them under a big bush. There! Now he had done his job. He would send in the bill to Mr Sailor Doll and get a great deal of money.

"I might almost have enough to pay for a new bicycle now," he thought, and he drove off at top speed. He got a passenger on the way back, a little toy horse who had such a long tail that hung down right over the back of the car.

NODDY PUT THE SACKS ONE BY ONE IN HIS LITTLE CAR

"It might get caught in the wheels," said Noddy anxiously. "Can't you tie it round your neck or something?"

"That's not the way to treat a tail like mine," said the toy horse, offended.

"All right! Let it sweep the road clean if you want it to!" said Noddy. "Here we go!"

―✺ 6 ✺―

VISITORS AT NIGHT

NOW that night there came a knocking at the door. "Rat-a-tatta-tatta-TAT!" It sounded a very cross kind of knocking, and it made Noddy and Big-Ears jump.

"Who's that?" said Big-Ears, surprised. "It's very late for a visitor. I hope it's not anyone who wants you to take him out in your car, Noddy."

Noddy opened the door, the bell on his hat jingling in fright, because the knocking *had* sounded very fierce.

Oh dear! There was Mr Plod the policeman outside, and with him were the Sailor Doll and Mrs Minnie Monkey who lived next door to him.

They all looked very cross indeed. They came right in and the Sailor Doll slammed the door.

"Noddy," said Mr Plod. "I should just like to know what you've been up to today!"

"I don't know. Tell me," said Noddy, trembling.

"Did you, or did you not, go to Ahoy Cottage today and steal six sacks from Mr Sailor Doll's shed?" asked Mr Plod, very solemnly, taking out his big black notebook as he spoke.

"I did go to his shed. But I didn't steal the sacks," said Noddy.

"Oh, the naughty little storyteller!" cried Mrs Monkey. "He came when Mr Sailor Doll was

out, and I *saw* him dragging the sacks out of the shed! Oh, the bad little fellow!"

"Well, Mr Sailor Doll sent me a message to take them out of his shed and drive to Red Goblin Corner and leave them there for his uncle!" cried Noddy.

"WHAT HAVE YOU BEEN UP TO TODAY?" ASKED MR PLOD

"Oh, I didn't!" said the Sailor Doll. "I didn't, I didn't, I didn't, I di–"

"That's enough 'didn'ts'," said Mr Plod. "I'm surprised at you, making up a story like this! What HAVE you done with the sacks? Are they here?"

Big-Ears suddenly rang the bicycle bell beside him very loudly indeed. It made everyone jump, and they all looked round.

"Let *me* speak!" said Big-Ears angrily. "How *dare* you call little Noddy names? How dare you say hc steals things? How dare you say that–"

"Be quiet," said Mr Plod crossly.

"I shan't be quiet!" yelled Big-Ears, and his bandage suddenly slipped down over one eye.

"Mrs Tubby gave Noddy the message about fetching the sacks. I heard her! Fetch her in."

Mr Plod sent Mrs Minnie Monkey to fetch Mrs Tubby. Mr Tubby came too, looking very surprised.

Well, of course, Mrs Tubby said that she *had* given Noddy the message. A little goblin had met her out in the village and told her to ask Noddy to fetch the sacks.

"It's a plot!" cried the Sailor Doll. "That's what it is! A plot to steal my carrots and my turnips and my potatoes, and my swedes and my onions, and my – er, my, well, I can't really remember what was in the sixth sack."

"Your good manners, perhaps!" cried Big-Ears, very red in the face. "Coming to our house like this, and telling stories about Noddy and–"

"Sh!" said Mr Plod, flapping his notebook at Big-Ears. "I tell you *I'm* handling this case. The thing is – Noddy took the sacks and he's to blame. Noddy, I'm afraid you must pay fifteen shillings to Mr Sailor Doll, this very minute. He's got to go to sea tomorrow, and he wants the money. He can't sell his sacks of vegetables now because they're gone."

Noddy wailed loudly. "But it WASN'T my fault! I did a lot of hard work and now I'm blamed for it and I've got to pay out all my money that I was saving up. Woo-hoo-hoo!"

"Well, don't pay it then," said Mr Plod. "But if you don't I'm afraid I must take you to prison for the night until this matter is cleared up."

"Pay the money. Don't you go to prison, Noddy!" cried Big-Ears. "I can't do without you, little Noddy, I can't, I can't!"

So poor little Noddy had to give up every penny in his money box to the Sailor Doll. Then Mr Plod went away with the doll and Mrs Monkey.

Noddy cried bitterly. Big-Ears comforted him. He whispered in his ear. "Noddy! Take your car and see if you can catch the thief at Red Goblin Corner! He may be coming at night to get the sacks! Go and catch him!"

7

NODDY IS VERY BRAVE

NODDY dried his eyes. He suddenly felt very fierce. "I'll catch him all right!" he said. "You just see!"

And off he went in his car, his new lamps shining very brightly indeed. But when he got to Red Goblin Corner he switched them off, and jumped out. He crept over to the bush where he had hidden the sacks.

Dear me, the sacks were still there! How marvellous! Was the thief coming to get them? If so, Noddy would jump out at him and give him the surprise of his life!

Noddy hid under the bush. He had taken a rope from his car. He took off his hat so that the bell wouldn't tinkle and give him away. He waited and he waited.

Sh! What was that! A little noise. And another little noise. And then a bigger noise. Then someone put a hand under the bush to feel if the sacks were there.

Noddy pounced. He caught the hand and leapt out of the bush.

He dragged the person to his car, and switched on the headlights.

"Good gracious!" he said, astonished. "It's Sly the Goblin! So it was *you* who played this horrid trick on me!"

He suddenly caught hold of the goblin's other hand. He tied both hands together with the rope. The goblin was a coward, and he fell on his knees at once.

"Mercy! Don't take me away with you. Don't take me to Mr Plod. It was only a joke. I tell you it was really only a joke."

"Ho! A joke, was it!" said Noddy fiercely. "Well, I nearly went to prison for your joke – and I've had to give up every penny out of my money box for your nasty joke. I've a good mind to tie you behind my car and drag you all the way to Mr Plod!"

"No, no, no!" squealed Sly.

"Or else I'll tie you on the front and drive straight into the pond," said Noddy, enjoying himself.

"MERCY! DON'T TAKE ME TO MR PLOD," CRIED SLY
THE GOBLIN

"No, no no!" squealed the goblin again. "Noddy, I'm sorry. Don't punish me. You've got the sacks, haven't you? You can take them back."

"Yes, but I've given all my money to the Sailor Doll, and he's going to sea so I shan't get it back," said Noddy. "And I'm sure Mr Plod won't let me sell what's in the sacks. No, no – I think I'll certainly punish you. I'll –"

"Please!" wept the goblin. "Please listen to me. Let me do a spell for you. I'm good at spells. Isn't there anything you want?"

"Nothing," said Noddy. But then he suddenly stopped and thought. Wait a minute – there *was* something he wanted – and wanted very badly, too!

"Have you a spell to make a bicycle exactly like the one that Big-Ears used to ride?" he asked.

"Big-Ears' bicycle was smashed to bits," said Sly. "If I had one of the bits I might work a spell on it to grow a bicycle just like Big-Ears used to have. But not a bit of it was left, so people say."

"There *is* something left of it!" cried Noddy. "The bell's left! Get into my car, Sly. I'll take

you straight back. And if you can really work a bicycle spell, I'll forgive you and let you go. Get in. I'm just going to put the sacks in the car, too."

So into the car got Sly the Goblin, trembling so much that the car shook, too. How frightened he was of fierce little Noddy!

8

THE WONDERFUL SPELL

NODDY put in all the sacks, and some of them went on top of Sly, who didn't like it at all. But he really didn't dare to say a word.

Then off they went, and soon came to Noddy's little house. Noddy dragged Sly out of the car and rushed him up to the front door. He opened it and in they went.

Big-Ears leapt up in surprise. "What's this? Who's that? You made me jump!"

"Where's your bicycle bell?" cried Noddy, so excited that he really couldn't answer any questions. "Oh, there it is. Big-Ears, watch! Something wonderful may be going to happen!"

Noddy put the bell down in front of Sly. He pointed at him. "Now, what about that spell? Go on, do it – or off to Mr Plod you go!"

Sly touched the bell with his foot. Then he leapt lightly around it. He chanted a curious little song:

"Bell, bell,
I weave you a spell,
Bicycle-magic is in it.
Grow, grow,
Two wheels in a row,
It won't take you more than a minute!
Make, make,
Pedals and brake,
Tyres and handle-bar too.
Bell, bell,
I weave you a spell,
Hollabee, rinnabee, HOOOOO!"

The last "HOOOOO" was so loud that Noddy and Big-Ears jumped, and Whiskers the cat fled under the bed. But my goodness me, what a spell that was!

The bicycle grew under their very eyes! Yes, it grew wheels and bars and pedals and brakes, fat tyres and even a big lamp in front! Big-Ears rushed to it in the greatest delight, and leapt on it. He began to cycle round and round the room, almost knocking little Noddy down.

"My bicycle's all right again! It's just the very same except that the lamp is bigger. Where's my bell? I'll put it on. There − now I can ring it too. R–r–r–ring! R–r–r–ring! R–r–r–ring!"

What excitement there was. Noddy was simply delighted to see that Big-Ears was quite himself again. He danced up and down and sang.

At last Big-Ears got off the bicycle and looked at Noddy, panting. "Where's that goblin?" he said. "I just want to give him one or two spanks for luck."

BIG-EARS BEGAN TO CYCLE ROUND AND ROUND THE
ROOM

But Sly had gone. He had slipped out quietly and was running as if a hundred dogs were after him. Dear, dear, to think that he had nearly been taken off to Mr Plod!

Mr and Mrs Tubby heard the bicycle bell ringing madly as Big-Ears raced around the room again, with Noddy on his shoulders this time. They came to see what the matter was.

How pleased they were! Big-Ears threw his bandage into the fire. Noddy took off his hat and rang the bell loudly in joy.

"Everything's come right!" he said. "Well – not *quite* everything." He suddenly looked solemn.

"What hasn't come right?" asked Big-Ears.

"Well – I planted a peppermint drop, a bull's-eye and a toffee," said Noddy. "Out in the garden, you know. I thought they'd grow into lovely little trees and I'd be able to sell the sweets that grew on them, just like Mr Wobbly sells the plums off his plum tree. But they didn't come up."

"Oh, you dear, funny little Noddy!" cried Mrs Tubby, and she gave him a hug.

"You silly, generous little fellow!" said Mr Tubby.

"Best friend in the world!" said Big-Ears, and smiled all over his big red face. "Who cares what happens, so long as we've got one another? Hurrah for little Noddy!"

And, dear me, Big-Ears suddenly burst into a little song, just as Noddy often did.

"Who is the best of us all?
Answer, everybody!
Someone very shy and small?
Why it's little Noddy!
Here he is with hat of blue,
Bell a-jingling all day through,
Smiling funny smiles at you,
Hullo, little Noddy!"

Well, wasn't that nice? Noddy was so pleased that he rushed at Big-Ears and nearly knocked him off his bicycle as he rode round and round the room.

Funny little Noddy. See you again sometime!